For Palma, who sees beauty in everything
—J. T.

To Carolina, Fernando, and Renata
—M. A.

Text copyright © 2004 by Joe Troiano
Illustrations copyright © 2004 by Martha Avilés
Design by Jeff Batzli
2004 Barnes & Noble Books

ISBN 0-7607-3505-0

Printed in China

10 9 8 7 6 5 4 3 2 1

It's Your Cloud

JOE TROIANO

ILLUSTRATIONS BY
MARTHA AVILÉS

BARNES & NOBLE BOOKS

NEW YORK

It's your cloud.
It can be what you like—
a moose playing baseball
or a mouse on a bike.

It's your cloud
and no two are alike—
there's a zebra with spots
and a leopard with stripes.

There's a beagle, a bagel, a butterfly.
The strangest things go fluttering by.

Some clouds have silver linings.
Some rain on parades.
Some run from the sun,
and some give us shade.

But the best clouds of all put on a show,
changing their shape
as they drift and they blow.
Shifting their shape into . . .
well . . . you never do know.

Is it a noodle with freckles
or a pickle with feet?

Is it a nickel with speckles
or a bicycle seat?

Is it a whatchamacallit
or a thingamajig
or a porcupine dancing on the head of a pig?

It's your cloud,
so don't be surprised
if it changes its shape
right in front of your eyes.

First it's a teapot.
Then it's a boat.

Then, abracadabra!
A fish in a coat.

Then a mitten,
then a muffin,
then a pumpkin pie,
and just when you think
you've seen every cloud in the sky . . .

. . . the strangest one of all blows by.

It's big.
It's small.
It's tiny.
It's tall.
It's any shape and every shape and no shape at all . . .

. . . because it's *your* cloud.
Watch it and see!
It can be whatever you want it to be—
anything at all
from A to Z,
from one to one million gazillion and three.

The possibilities are endless.
Every shape is allowed.
If you want, it can even look like . . .
a cloud!